WRESTLING WITH THE CHAMP:

BETTER RED THAN DEAD

About the Show:

Born in a thunderstorm during 2020, Wrestling with The Champ is the funniest ride in wrestling, starring Ant McGinley (The Champ AKA The Ginger Ninja) and Damien St John (Himself).

Better Red than Dead was first performed at the Leicester Comedy Festival in 2022, and later at the OmniCentre, Edinburgh Fringe Festival as part of the PBH Free Fringe.

Thanks to everyone who showed up to cheer us on, shelter from the Scottish rain or joined in the fun on the streets of Edinburgh during an unforgettable summer. Special thanks to: Jeffrey Walker, Sean Allsop, The Muir Family, Tom Campbell, plus our friends and families for putting up with this crazy side hustle adventure.

Look out for more live dates at www.wrestlingwiththechamp.com

Stream every episode now on Apple Podcasts, Spotify, Audible, Google Podcasts, Castbox and other awesome podcast providers.

Copyright © 2023 Damien St John and Ant McGinley. All rights reserved. No part of this publication may be reproduced, distributed, or transmitted in any form or by any means, including photocopying, recording, or other electronic or mechanical methods, without the prior written permission of the publisher, except as permitted by copyright law. For permission requests, visit www.wrestlingwiththechamp.com. The story, all names, characters, and incidents portrayed in this production are fictitious. No identification with actual persons (living or deceased), places, buildings, and products is intended or should be inferred.

About the Authors:

Damien St John is a standup comedian and children's author. In 2017, Damien was awarded a place on the BAFTA Rocliffe TV Comedy Forum list and has since material broadcast on the BBC as part of the Radio 4 Extra programme, Newsjack. Damien is also a children's author, having published picture books for both his children. My Buddy is so Muddy and The Desert Duck are available now on Amazon.

Ant McGinley is a comedian, character actor and DJ. In 2019, he made the shortlist for the APA Production Awards Producer of the Year, and in 2017 received a Bronze Award for Best Sports Radio at the UK ARIAS. As well as being a host, producer, and coach, Ant is an international speaker on podcasts.

THIS PAGE IS LEFT INTENTIONALLY BLANK.

FEEL FREE TO DRAW A PICTURE OF YOURSELF.

THIS RIGHT-HAND PAGE IS LEFT INTENTIONALLY BLANK.

FILL YOUR BOOTS.

LIGHTS UP.

RAUCOUS ROCK MUSIC MUSIC ENDS.

DSJ ENTERS AND ADDRESSES THE CROWD.

> DSJ:
>
> Hello everyone and welcome to the most amazing, sensational, electrifying main event of your day here at the Edinburgh Fringe Festival as part of the PBH Free Fringe... It's the live adventures of the cult comedy podcast, Wrestling with The Champ! [PAUSE FOR CHEERS] I'm your host, Damien St John... Any listeners in the house tonight?

PAUSE FOR NO RESPONSE.

DSJ (CONT'D):

Always a leveler, that one. It's great to be here in person, finally... Our show was remote last year due to Covid. Did anyone see it? Good. It was shit. In a live demonstration, Mean Dean from Aberdeen tried to give himself an inverted atomic drop, but in the process, he fell on a door handle and managed to tear open his asshole.

PAUSE.

DSJ (CONT'D):

Speaking of asshole, your special guest tonight is a legendary wrestler, a force majeure of the Pub Wrestling Federation, and my co-host on Wrestling with The Champ with a career longer than an end user license agreement -- and the ego to match. And he is here, in his new show "Better Red than Dead" to reveal how he survived life in the squared circle. Everything you've ever wanted to know about life in the squared circle from the man who has seen it all, done it all, and been barred from most of the pubs in Scotland as a result... Are you ready? Are you ready?

DSJ (CONT'D):
[RING ANNOUNCER VOICE] Entering the ring, weighing significantly more than he did last week, let's call it carb-loading, he is the kung-fu kicking, karate

chopping legend himself, and the only man to have ever poked three women at once in a Kia Picanto, earning him the nickname "The Mick Hucknall of Wrestling"... Give it all up for the Ginger Ninja!

CROWD CHEERS.

MUSIC: SIMPLY RED – SOMETHING GOT ME STARTED

THE CHAMP ENTERS, TRIUMPHANTLY, FOR ALL THE CROWD TO SEE.

HE WAITS UNTIL HE'S CLEAR OF THE AUDIENCE BEFORE DOUSING HIMSELF IN A FULL CAN OF DEEP HEAT.

DSJ (CONT'D):

Sorry, Edinburgh. This is taking a stupidly long amount of time. Champ, come on. Hurry up!

THE CHAMP PADS IT OUT EVEN MORE BEFORE DAMIEN FINALLY CUTS THE MUSIC... BUT THE CHAMP CARRIES ON IN DEFIANCE, LEADING THE CROWD IN A CHANT.

CHAMP:

When I say Ginger, you say Ninja... Ginger [PAUSE FOR REPLY]... When I Say 'The' you say Champ... The [PAUSE FOR REPLY]... When I say 'Dinner' you say Yes... Dinner [PAUSE FOR REPLY].

DSJ:

Come on!

THE CHAMP MERRILY JOGS TO THE STAGE TO SAY HIS GOODBYES.

> CHAMP:
>
> I've scored there... Thank you, Scotland!
>
> Good night!

THE CHAMP MOTIONS TO WALK OFF WHEN –

> DSJ:
>
> [CONFUSED] Sorry... Err... What are you doing? I booked you for 45 minutes.

THE CHAMP PUTS DSJ IN A HEADLOCK.

> CHAMP:
>
> Damo... Damo... Damo...!

DSJ:

[CONSTRICTED] Err... Yes...?

CHAMP:

Did you say 45 minutes or four to five minutes?

DSJ:

[CONSTRICTED] Definitely 45 minutes.

THE CHAMP GLEEFULLY TIGHTENS HIS HEADLOCK.

DSJ (CONT'D):

[CONSTRICTED] Let... Me... Go--

THE CHAMP SLOWLY AND SUSPICIOUSLY EASES OFF.

DSJ (CONT'D):

[GASPS] These people are here to witness a once-in-a-lifetime interview with you, a bonafide pub wrestling legend.

CHAMP:

Ha ha. Boner.

DSJ:

Can we work something out?

CHAMP:

[QUICKLY] Cover me bar bill and we're golden. Deal?

DSJ

Deal. Let's get cracking. First up, let me ask you, Champ--

CHAMP INTERRUPTS DAMO AND REMOVES HIS CLOAK.

          CHAMP:

—-Hello, love. [POINTS TO THE BAR] I'll have a Full Nelson Over the Ropes, an Espresso Martini Neckbreaker, two Tequila Power-slammers and a Vodka Tonic with a Twist of Fate. What's your poison, big dick?

          DSJ:

I'll just have milk, actually.

          CHAMP:

[DEFINITIVE] --Like fuck. You'll have Sweet Gin Music. Extra absinthe. Smack on top. Don't hold back on the Baileys.

DSJ:

Do you normally drink that after a show?

CHAMP:

Do I fuck. [PROUD] But this is a special occasion... I'm in Edinburgh. Birthplace of Lady in Red singer Chris De Burgh where I have laid many an opponent to rest. [BRAGGING] I've laid a few fans too. Shout out to Sharon if she's in tonight!

DSJ:

Nice outfit. [TO THE AUDIENCE] This is what happens when you order a wrestler from Wish. Now, Champ, you always stay true to your ninja roots by wearing something black – Talk us through all the blacks you've wrestled in.

CHAMP:

Oh aye. Dark black. Light black. Grey black. Midnight black. Liquorice black. Mold black. Penguin black. Matt Black. Jack Black. Black hole black. Black ice black. Darth Vader black. Dark Knight black, Black History Month black, HDMI cable black… And Noir.

DSJ:

So why did you call this show "Better Red than Dead"?

CHAMP:

Even though I've been "Gingered" more times than a Ron Weasley lookalike at a Harry Potter convention, I wouldn't change a thing. I'm a certified, strawberry-blonde winner and unlike the gingerbread man, if you bite me, I bite back. And only now, in my old age, do I realise how much I've had to give up to get here - because I'm ginger. The scars on my body and mind... Oh, those chair shots... I've lost count of the number of concussions...

DSJ:

–Nine.

CHAMP:

I've lost count of the number of bones I've smashed just to keep hold of the belt for a few more weeks.

DSJ:

732.

CHAMP:

The backhanders I've taken to lose matches.

DSJ:

17.

CHAMP:

The people that trusted me, who I later betrayed...

DSJ:

493—

CHAMP:

[CUTS DAMO OFF, SOFTLY]--Don't.

DSJ:

What do you love most about wrestling?

CHAMP:

I've been asked that a lot over the years, and my answer is always the same... The fans.

DSJ:

Such a great answer. Wrestling needs its fans. As we saw during the pandemic, without a crowd showing up each week, it's just two blokes in an empty room touching each other for money.

CHAMP:

I have also done that show.

DSJ:

What do you say to the anti-gingers?

CHAMP:

My record speaks for itself. I've got more wins than Federer... More gold than the Brink's Mat Robbers... And more titles than Hamilton, Murray, Farah and Flintoff combined. And can any of them say they've won a naked pudding match?

DSJ & CHAMP:

[BOTH, AGREES] Flintoff.

DSJ:

You're a veteran. You've been around. Wrestling doesn't get any easier. Look at Ric Flair. Last match at 73. But the PWF has a problem, though, hasn't it?

CHAMP:

The "Pwoof"? Can't say that these days, Damo. You'll go straight to HR.

DSJ:

No– Young people aren't drinking. Beer sales are down, pubs are closing. As the Pub Wrestling Federation champion, an icon of an era, that makes you a dying breed, doesn't it?

CHAMP WALKS AMONGST THE CROWD, SHAKING HANDS AS HE DRIFTS BETWEEN PEOPLE, ALMOST POLITICIAN-LIKE.

          CHAMP:

[SCOFFS] Au contrere mon Cher. In fact, the only thing more wrong than that naive statement is a cauliflower steak. Pubs, and pub wrestling, are booming. Night after night, we fight up and down the UK, entertaining pissheads and barflies. Proper sport for proper people. Ask anyone who's been to one of my shows, and they'll say the same thing about me. "Unbeatable. Astonishing. In a class of his own. Finger-fuck maestro...".

THE CHAMP HOLDS THE GAZE OF ONE AUDIENCE MEMBER FOR TOO LONG.

>	DSJ:

>	You've come from nothing. No offence to anyone from Rochdale, but surely that means anyone can become a wrestler?

>	CHAMP:

Funny you mention that... With the right trainer and £240... No, £340... I can make anyone's dreams come true. So let's be crazy. Come on, let's do it!

>	DSJ:

Do what?

CHAMP:

A crash course in wrestling! Who's up for it?

DSJ:

I'm not sure the OMNi Centre is insured for this...

Take the Wee Blue Book or the referee gets it.

The gun show on show inside stage 4

Back to back and side by side through it all

And I will always hurt you 🎶

Hypnotic, isn't he?

Hulking up or constipated? You decide.

Damien failed to control Ant yet again. This time at a busy Edinburgh junction.

(L) The official Better Red Than Dead flyer image. (R) General Confusion, The Champ's moniker during a tour of British Army bases in 2011 dubbed the "Balls up in the Barracks".

Deep in thought about beer, snacks that accompany beer and how to beat the fruit machine.

DEEP HEAT
DOG TAGS
VEST ~~HAVE~~ PRESENT TO RIP

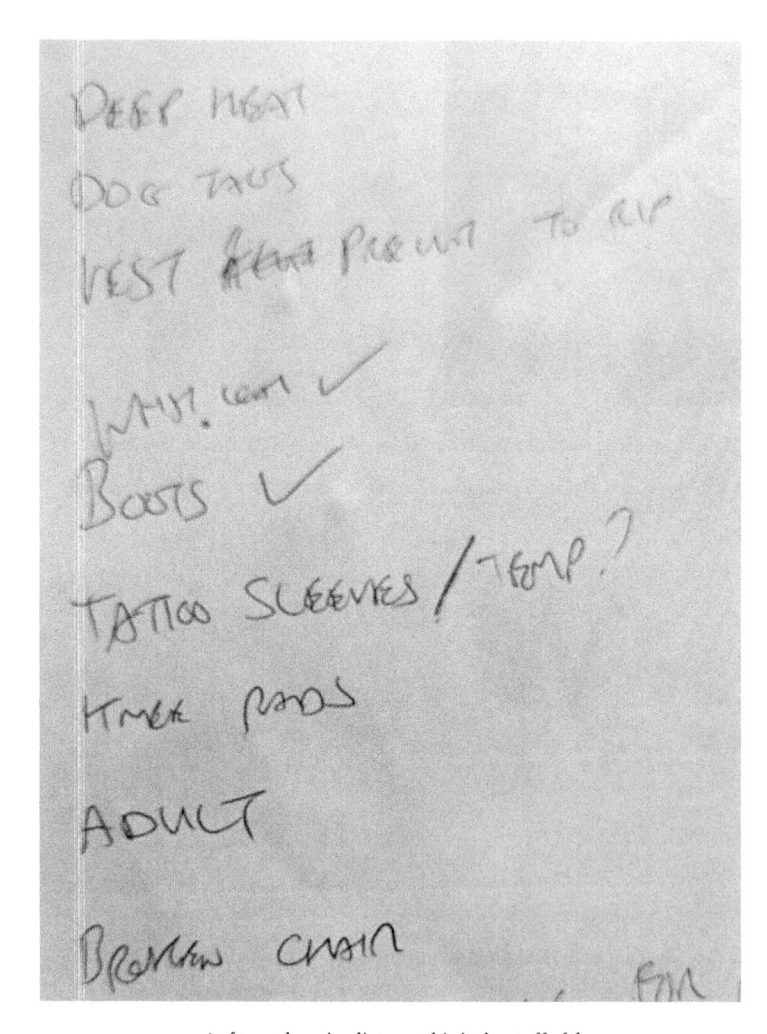

WHM.com ✓
BOOTS ✓

TATTOO SLEEVES / TEMP?

KNEE PADS

ADULT

BROKEN CHAIN

FAR

As far as shopping lists go, this is the stuff of dreams.

Paper-thin, plywood walls. A bedsheet held up with masking tape and a stain-soaked stage. We can promise it doesn't get much worse than this.

Has there ever been a less awkward pose? We think not.

The Champ in his happy place doing stickers and flyers.

Two iconic looks. One low price tag.

THE CHAMP LOOKS AT THE CROWD.

> CHAMP:
>
> I see lots of potential. Who wants to become a real wrestler like me? Come on!

CHAMP PICKS SOMEONE FROM THE CROWD. CROWD CHEERS.

MUSIC: JOE ESPOSITO - YOU'RE THE BEST (FADES, THEN)

> CHAMP (CONT'D):
>
> What's your name? Where are you from? What do you do for a living?

PUNTER ANSWERS.

CHAMP:

To get to the top in the PWF... And I'm assuming that you DO want to compete for the UK's premiere wrestling promotion..? Good. For me to make you a star, you need three things. Oh, hang on... Totally forgot the most important question of them all... Have you got the cash? It was £340. We accept contactless, or Ko-fi. No? Don't worry. I'll shake you down for it on the way out. [BACK TO TALKING TO THE AUDIENCE] Now. First? You need a ring walk to set the tone and intimidate your opponent. So let's see what you've got... Walk to me like you mean business...

CHAMP DIRECTS PUNTER TO WALK TOWARDS HIM MENACINGLY — AND AFTERWARDS OFFERS CRITICAL FEEDBACK, PERHAPS USING PUNTER'S JOB FOR WALK MOTIVATION E.G. "WALK TO ME LIKE I'M JOE FROM ACCOUNTS AND I HAVEN'T PAID YOUR INVOICE."

THEN:

> CHAMP (CONT'D):
> Next it's your signature pose. Now this needs to be memorable. Try this one. Copy me. Do everything I do. Got it?

THE CHAMP PUMPS HIMSELF UP, GIVING AN ALMIGHTY PEP TALK TO HIMSELF AS HE DOES... WHEN HE'S READY TO BURST HE RACES TOWARDS THE AUDIENCE AND ROARS AS HE RIPS HIS SHIRT OPEN.

CHAMP (CONT'D):

[MATTER OF FACT] Now your turn.

UNSURPRISINGLY, THE PUNTER DOESN'T FOLLOW, SO THE CHAMP CHECKS LABEL FOR MANUFACTURER.

CHAMP (CONT'D):

Oh right... [SAYS NAME OF BRAND]

Probably an expensive one. Nevermind,

let's sort out your finishing move.

DSJ:

And tell us about yours, Champ.

CHAMP:

Mine is an inverted atomic piledriver.

called 'Crushing Reality.' If you're

wondering how I got the name, it's a

proper emotional one... [THE CHAMP WELLS UP] I went to the bank many years ago when my career were on the ropes and I couldn't pay my Sky Sports bill. I asked 'em for a loan, they said 'no'. And that were a [EMOTIONAL] Crushing Reality.

AWKWARD SILENCE.

CHAMP (CONT'D):

[TO PUNTER] Has anything sad like that ever happened to you? [PAUSE FOR REPLY]. Well... The finisher that would be perfect for you, is The Fresh Prints.

DSJ:

What's that?

CHAMP:

It's where you slap your opponent so hard that you leave print marks... Hey, if it's good enough for Will Smith, it'll do for you. But slap me on the back, not the face, I've just had dental work. Now, let's see you put it all together.

CHAMP DIRECTS the PUNTER TO PUT EVERYTHING TOGETHER IN ONE FLUID ACTION - WALK, POSE + SHIRT RIP AND FINISHER.

CHAMP (CONT'D):

[LOUDLY] Come on... Finish me off! Give me The Fresh Prints.

THE PUNTER WHACKS CHAMP ON THE BACK WITH AN ALMIGHTY THUMP – IT LANDS HARD. THE CHAMP SELLS IT WELL.

CHAMP (CONT'D):
Jesus H Samuel... You could properly hurt someone doing that. Good though, stronger than you look. Wanna selfie?

CHAMP TAKES SELFIE WITH THE PUNTER ON-STAGE.

CHAMP:
That'll be £12.

DSJ:
That has hopefully set you on your way to becoming a PWF superstar one day if you pay your subs. Thank you... Punter!

MUSIC: JOE ESPOSITO - YOU'RE THE BEST (FADES)

CROWD APPLAUSE. PUNTER EXITS.

> CHAMP:
>
> [CHAMP COUNTS HIS EARNINGS] Hey. What are you doing a week on Tuesday? Got a spot at The Rose and Bush in Runcorn. [BLOWING] I need a drink after that.

CHAMP NECKS A CAN OF DRINK HIDDEN IN HIS BELT - BUT KEEPS THE CAN NEARBY.

A BEAT.

DSJ:

You've spent your entire career in the Pub Wrestling Federation... Were the big leagues something you regret not joining?

CHAMP:

What the fuck are you talking about? I am in the big leagues! Who else can sell out Wetherspoons, O'Neills and the occasional Harvester night after night AND say they went to number 74 in the Israeli charts with their debut album?

DSJ & CHAMP:

[BOTH AGREE] Flintoff...

DSJ:

I'd forgotten about 1997's "Refrain from the Pain."

CHAMP:

Let me remind you of some of the songs... A Boy Named Suplex...? Wichita Clotheslineman...? She Piledrives Me Crazy...? And that one Phil Collins took me to court over... Su-su-su-Suplexio! Hey, shall we give it a go?

DSJ:

Err, I'm not sure we should...?

CHAMP:

Come on, it'll be a blast. Everyone up on their feet.

44

THE CHAMP MOTIONS THE AUDIENCE TO STAND.

MUSIC: PHIL COLLINS - SUSSUDIO

CHAMP:

Right. Hands on hips, copy me. Keep up!

THE CHAMP LEADS THE AUDIENCE IN AN ENERGETIC DANCE ROUTINE. ITS CLIMAX SEES THE CHAMP OPENING A DRINKS CAN, STICKING TO HIS HEAD, AND POURING IT INTO A PINT GLASS.

Pour some fizzy on me 🎵 (no drinks company endorses this photo)

CHAMP:

Hey. I do poetry too. "Some people they call me quite blunt, and some people they call me a c--"

DSJ:

--Carrying on. Now, we all know that wrestling is... Well, it's scripted.

CHAMP:

Yeah, it is. But don't say it's fake. If you say it's fake I'll crush you quicker than an empty can of Irn-Bru.

DSJ:

[BACKING OFF] Hey. I know it's real, you know it's real. It is REAL.

CHAMP:

Pain? Real. Sweat? Real. B.O.--

DSJ:

[GAGS] Ugh--Very real.

THE CHAMP GOES TO MOON THE CROWD.

CHAMP:

The open wound where the stepladder nearly went up me arse--

DSJ:

--Would you put that away! Can you tell these lovely people a true story about wrestling being real that doesn't involve you getting your knob out...?

CHAMP:

[THINKS, THEN, CONFIDENTLY] Err... No. Why don't you tell 'em some of your favourite matches of mine? I'm sick of doing all the storytelling.

DSJ:

Okay, let's think. My top three Ginger Ninja matches... First, The Screw Job where you beat Captain Cambridge for the Bar Fly title. You screwed him, literally, when you swapped all the steel screws holding the cage together before the match for tin ones. Tin has a much lower melting point than steel, so melted in the heat as the temperature in the room rose. Genius. Also disturbing.

CHAMP:

Cheat or get beat. That's my motto.

DSJ:

[CONCERNED] Do you feel any remorse? He ended up in a wheelchair.

CHAMP:

[SCOFFS] He won't be coming for a rematch tonight. This place lacks an accessible entrance.

DSJ:

Then there was the infamous Steak and Wail night. I'll never forget it. I remember a rogue chip pan fire broke out just minutes before your main event.

CHAMP:

That were fun. When the fire brigade turned up, all the old ladies in the front row thought the lads were strippers and started aggressively grinding on their breathing apparatus.

DSJ:

And the time you force your way onto the bill at the PWF's first all-female show...

CHAMP:

[NOSTALGIC] Wrestle Labia... Fun times.

DSJ:

[CRINGES] You broke a wrestling record that night with over 200 pin attempts.

CHAMP:

I do whatever it takes to be on top.

DSJ:

Speaking of being "on top." Edinburgh is the city of love--

CHAMP:

[BLUSHES] It's the hair, isn't it? Got you fired up for a bit of roleplay, you dirty dog? You're cute but I wouldn't. Not even from behind.

DSJ:

During your long career, did you ever make time to find "the one"? Someone to do long-term sex tag with?

CHAMP:

Many've knocked on the door [KNOCKS ON CROTCH BOX] but few have been let in.

DSJ:

Because of your status?

CHAMP:

No. Me name.

DSJ:

Your name?

CHAMP:

Oh aye. Nobody wants to fuck a Nigel. A boring name is one of life's great burdens —And wrestlers are particularly troubled.

DSJ:

Oh yeah? Like who?

CHAMP:

Hulk Hogan? Real name's Terry. The Rock? He's Dwayne. CM Punk's a Phillip. 'Stone Cold' Steve Austin? [PAUSE] Just regular Steve. Women want a gent in the street but a wrestler in the bed. Throw 'em around a bit, you know? Suplex off the wardrobe, piledriver with your penis – Sharon! If you're in, call me!

DSJ:

Now we're getting to the juicy truth!

CHAMP:

Trust me. As the Champ, the sort of kinky shit I've done would make Russell Brand's knob blush. But as Nigel? I've seen less action than the Canadian army.

Photo: A cannon in Canada, last fired circa Christmas 1873.

THE CHAMP TAKES HIS WIG OFF AND GETS REAL.

>   CHAMP:
>
>   Whenever this wig comes OFF, those knickers stay ON. It's why so many "professional" wrestlers are assholes. And that's my advice to any aspiring superstars. If you're all about getting your end away, never EVER break character, or you'll find yourself in a Travelodge every night wanking alone.

THE CHAMP SUBTLE WIPES HIS RIGHT HAND ON HIS TROUSERS – BEFORE PUTTING HIS WIG BACK ON.

>   DSJ:
>
>   So, there's no love interest?

CHAMP:

No. I'm a dying breed.

DSJ:

Alpha male chauvinist gammon–?

CHAMP:

[DEFENSIVE] --Gammon is NOT an insult! No. Nobody's calling their babies "Nigel". So, even if I did find someone to settle down with, there'd be no Nigel Junior.

DSJ:

What about Nigella?

CHAMP:

[GRUNTS] Oh, I definitely would.

DSJ:

You do know that Nigella is the feminine version of Nigel...?

CHAMP:

[UPSET] Why have you got to ruin everything? How can I beat me eggs off to her now, knowing she's got my name? [PAUSE] Hey, that could work...!

DSJ:

What?

CHAMP:

Telly show idea... Nigel's Kitchen!
[PRONOUNCED NIGE-HELLS] The PWF

champion cooks his favourite recipes in front of a live studio audience of sexy, excitable fans.

DSJ:
What are you going to cook?

CHAMP:
Coque au Champ. My signature dish. Like a signature move but nicer on the palette. Speaking of which... Ginger snack?

THE CHAMP CRACKS OPEN THE SNACKS - MAYBE GINGER NUTS - AND INHALES THEM LIKE THE COOKIE MONSTER.

DSJ:
What's in Coq au Champ?

CHAMP:

[MOUTH FULL] Chicken, tarragon and creme fraiche, simmered in a pint of my award-winning alcoholic energy drink, Champain.

DSJ:

You can't call it Champain...!

CHAMP:

Why not? I'm the Champ and I'm all about "the pain." Champain!

DSJ:

Trading standards will be all over you for that.

CHAMP:

Then bring it on! They can't touch Champain. It's got celebrity fans.

DSJ:

Like who?

CHAMP:

Mrs. Hinch. She uses it to unlock her drains—

AT SOME POINT, THE CHAMP STARTS CHOKING.

DSJ:

Champ…? Are you alright? Champ?

CHAMP:

[CHOKING] No, you fucking dick… I'm choking.

DSJ:

Maybe it was the ginger nuts. Is there a ginger nut stuck in your throat?

UNABLE TO BREATHE, THE CHAMP GASPS DESPERATELY.

DSJ (CONT'D):

Shit. Shit! Oh, no, please don't die.

CHAMP:

[CHOKES] Help! Help!

THE CHAMP PANICS AND TRIES TO CLEAR HIS THROAT BY NECKING A PINT BUT IT'S NO GOOD.

HE STILL CAN'T BREATHE.

DSJ:

I knew I should've booked the Iron Sheikh. Fuck. Err... Is there a doctor in the house? A paramedic? Anyone who's seen Casualty? Grey's Anatomy?

IT'S CLEAR THAT THE CHAMP IS ABOUT TO DIE.

HE STRUGGLES TO POINT TO THE PUNTER FROM THE IMPROV SECTION -- AND MIMES A LIFE-SAVING MOVE.

CHAMP:

[CHOKES] Argh... Quick...

THE AUDIENCE ISN'T SURE WHETHER TO LAUGH OR PANIC. MAYBE THEY DO BOTH.

DSJ:

[LIGHTBULB MOMENT] Of course! You! Person! You can do it. You can do it...! Come on! Save the Champ!

DSJ ENCOURAGES THE PUNTER TO GET BACK ON STAGE AND SAVE THE CHAMP BY PERFORMING HIS NEWLY-LEARNED FINISHING MOVE.

A BEAT WHILE DAMO CUES THE ENTRANCE MUSIC, THEN GETS THE PUNTER TO PUT A T-SHIRT ON A RIP IT BEFORE DOING A 3-2-1 COUNTDOWN.

MEANWHILE, THE CHAMP IS TURNING BLUE.

A BEAT... THEN THE PUNTER LEANS IN AND PERFORMS THE FRESH PRINTS ON THE CHAMP!

GINGER NUTS SHOOT FROM THE CHAMP'S MOUTH AND HIT DSJ. AS THE CHAMP GASPS FOR AIR, THE CROWD APPLAUD.

>DSJ (CONT'D):
>
> Wow! I don't think I've seen that before. Probably the first time someone has a) been saved by a wrestling move, and b) saved by the person they just taught that wrestling move to. Incredible!

>CHAMP:
>
> [GASPS] That were close... The closest I've been to dying since Sharon accidentally pegged me in the wrong hole... Damo... Damo... I've seen the light.

DSJ:

What do you mean?

CHAMP:

Everything you said about how much of a terrible person I am… It's true. All of it.

DSJ:

So you've seen the error of your ways and start to live a softer, gentler life? Great!

CHAMP:

No, you numpty. I'm not the Andrex fucking puppy. I'm getting a top agent. These edgy stories could help me crack Hollywood. Damian Lewis could play me.

DSJ:

Kevin the Carrot could play you. We came here tonight to learn the truth about surviving life in the squared circle, and we've just witnessed it for ourselves. [TO PUNTER] You JUST saved a man from dying tonight... How does it feel?

PUNTER RESPONDS.

CHAMP:

Can I just say something?

DSJ:

Go for it.

THE CHAMP ADDRESSES THE CROWD.

CHAMP:

For that act of selflessness in the face of danger, I'd like to crown you the official PWF Underdog Champion! What do you reckon?!

PUNTER RESPONDS POSITIVELY.

CHAMP (CONT'D):

Good. Tap your card on the reader on the way out, and we'll send your belt parts in the post each month. Should be done in a year.

DSJ:

He's only joking.

CHAMP:

True. More like three years. The little belt screws get shipped from China.

DSJ:

--And that's it for the show. Thank you for supporting live comedy at the PBH Free Fringe. Enjoy tons of hows across the city this month. The shows are free, but putting them on isn't. We have to share a bedroom for ten nights straight. Comedy is not as glamorous as you might think! Given the fact our show is set in the Pub Wrestling Federation, we think we're worth the price of a pint. If you throw in the cost of a packet of spicy Nik Naks, you won't offend us. Download our podcast on Apple Podcasts, Spotify, Google, and all the good places. Champ?

CHAMP:

You've seen me cough up, now it's your turn... Please give generously!

THE END.

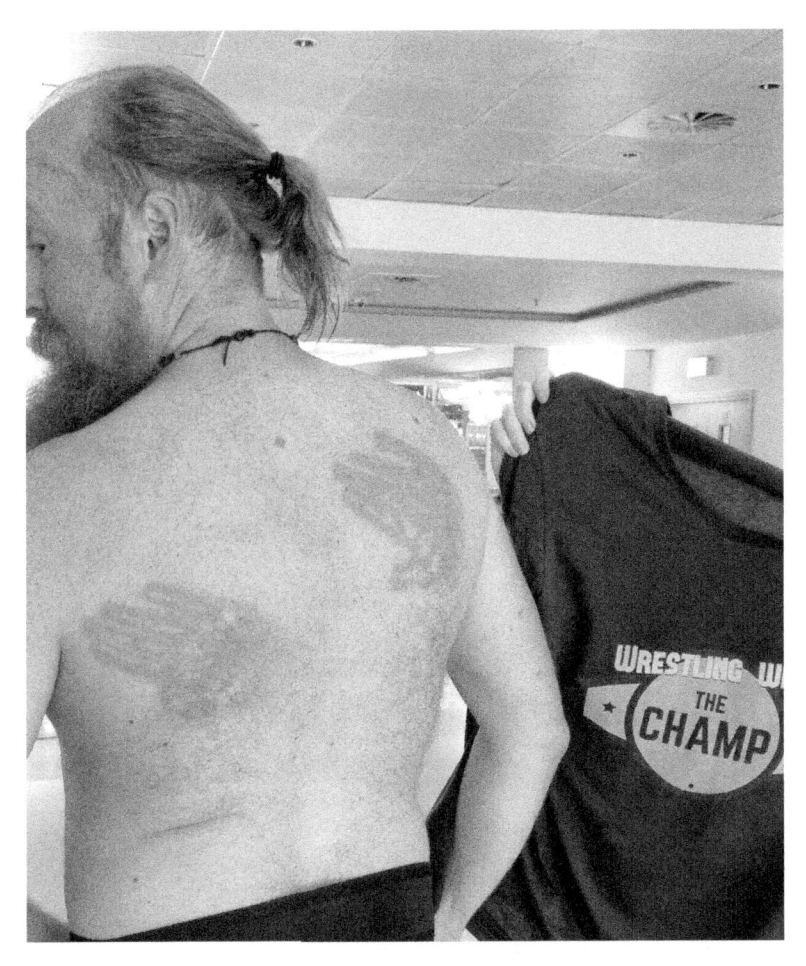

Who says fake wrestling is fake? Witness "The Fresh Prints".

Damien St John, Ant McGinley, John Robertson AKA The Dark Room

The Four Saucemen: Damien St John, Ian Skinner, Ant McGinley, VooDoo

Legend alert: Ant McGinley and Colin the Bar Manager at OmniVerse

s, Champ.

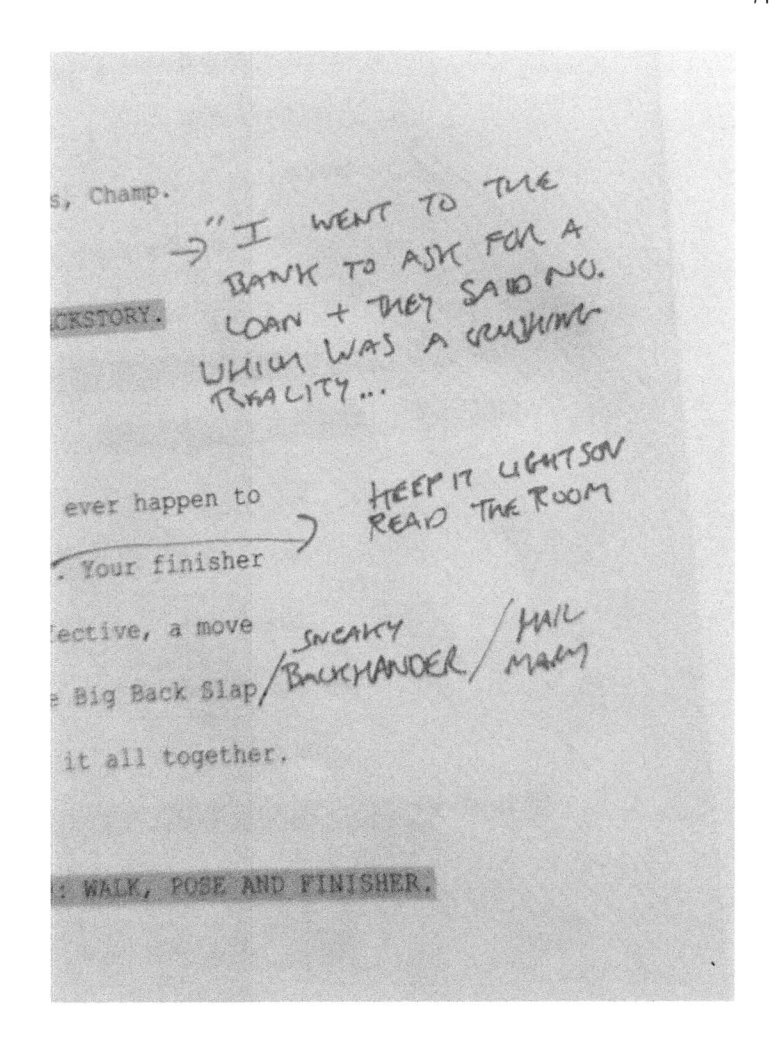

→ "I WENT TO THE BANK TO ASK FOR A LOAN + THEY SAID NO. WHICH WAS A CRUSHING REALITY..."

CKSTORY.

ever happen to ⎞ KEEP IT LIGHT SON
. Your finisher ⎠ READ THE ROOM

ective, a move   SNEAKY / HAIL
e Big Back Slap / BACKHANDER / MARY

it all together.

: WALK, POSE AND FINISHER.

One move. Many names. Multiple script changes.

SET : BISCUITS
BELT : PHONE. DEEP HEAT. IRN BRU

WRESTLING WITH THE CHAMP: BETTER READ TH

WARMUP MUSIC ENDS

DSJ IS ON STAGE - ON THE PHONE.

                        DSJ

No, no... You're late... You haven't g

time to shop at Jenners, we're on...

could've done this at half the pri

none of the hassle with The Iron

We've got a crowd in and... Yep, pe

Successfully localise the script for the locals by inserting nearby shop names.

A MASSIVE MUSCLE-SIZED THANKS TO EVERYONE WHO CONTRIBUTED TO OUR FIRST FOUR SEASONS, INCLUDING:

Adam Jarrell, Aimee Joshua, Alex Boardman, Alex Whitely, Alex VanTrue, Andrea Fox, Andrew Pickup, Andrew Wilson, Arywn Hughes, Ash Frith, Beccy Spurrit, Ben Hart, Caroline Verdon, Charles Commins, Ciaran Saward, Colin Christensen, Colin Leggo, Dan Maudsley, Dan Mellins-Cohen, David Scott, Dawn Bailey, Ego Mori, Harry Stachini, Hayley Cotter, Hayley Ellis, Ian Brannan, Jack Johnson, Jason Webster, Jeff Downs, Jim Salveson, Jo Milmine, Joey Rinaldi, John Walker, Jon Weeks, Jonny Goldsmith, Kevin Bennett, Kurt Cornwell, Lee Burton, Lewis Howley, Lewis Reeves, Lindsey Sykora, Max Cavenham, Megan Hayward, Mick Ferry, Mick Tully, Neal McClelland, Pat Sharp, Paul Jones, Paul McGinley, Phillip Simon, Rachel Graham, Rich Hall, Rob Tofield, Rob Verdon, Róisín Pope, Sam Stoker, Samuel Thomas, Sefanie Johnson, Tom Campbell, Tony Wright, Vic Turnbull, VooDoo and Wayne Allsop.

A CHAMPAHOLIC IS YOU!

WRESTLING WITH THE CHAMP

EPISODE GUIDE

SEASON ONE

- The Old Foe
- Father's Day
- The Royal Fumble
- Ma Ginger Monologues
- Once, Twice, Three Times a Champion
- The Pr*ck List
- Return of the PWF

WRESTLING WITH THE CHAMP

EPISODE GUIDE

SEASON TWO

- Où Est le Champ?
- The Vanishing Wrestler
- I Want to Wrestle Santa
- The Matchmaker
- The NWA and Pretty Deadly
- Scarred in the Yard
- Bruise Cruise

WRESTLING WITH THE CHAMP

EPISODE GUIDE

SEASON THREE

- Big Breaks
- The Hall of Flame
- Caravan of Hell
- Far Out in the Far East
- The GOATS
- The Final Bell – Part One
- The Final Bell – Part Two

WRESTLING WITH THE CHAMP

EPISODE GUIDE

SEASON FOUR

- Churros
- Night of The Ninja
- Tinseltown
- Kayfabe
- Bruise Willis
- Violence is Golden
- Blood is Thicker than Whiskey

OUT NOW!

PWF MAG

ISSUE 73
APRIL 23
£3 UK

EXCLUSIVE: CRABTREE SPEAKS!

KIDS EAT FREE AT PWF VENUES: VOUCHERS INSIDE

WHO IS THE LANDLORD? WE DISCUSS FAN THEORIES!

WHY GRANNIES NO LONGER GO TO WRESTLING SHOWS... REVEALED!

FOR MORE FROM 'WRESTLING WITH THE CHAMP'

VISIT OUR WEBSITE!

WRESTLINGWITHTHECHAMP.COM

OR SEARCH FOR US ON SOCIALS. WE'RE THERE. OR SCAN THIS SCANNY THING ON A HALF-DECENT PHONE.

Copyright © 2023 Damien St John and Ant McGinley. All rights reserved.